Mr Gum

Old Granny

Mr Gum in 'The Hound of Lamonic Bibber'

by Andy Stanton

Illustrated by
David Tazzyman

Polly

Martin
Launderette

Friday O'Leary

Billy William
the Third

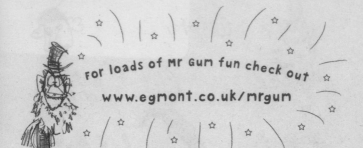

For loads of Mr Gum fun check out

www.egmont.co.uk/mrgum

Also by Andy Stanton:

You're A Bad Man, Mr Gum!

Mr Gum and the Biscuit Billionaire

Mr Gum and the Goblins

Mr Gum and the Power Crystals

Mr Gum and the Dancing Bear

EGMONT

We bring stories to life

First published 2009 by Egmont UK Limited, 239 Kensington High Street London W8 6SA

Text copyright © 2009 Andy Stanton
Illustration copyright © 2009 David Tazzyman

The moral rights of the author and illustrator have been asserted

ISBN 978 0 9559 4462 8

1 3 5 7 9 10 8 6 4 2

A CIP catalogue record for this title is available from the British Library

Printed in the UK by CPI Bookmarque, Croydon, CR0 4TD

Chapter 1

Terror in the Fog

Swirl, swirl, swirl.

The fog snaked its way through the midnight streets of Lamonic Bibber, thick and cold, and silent as an assassin.

Swirl, swirl, swirl.

The fog crept up to Boaster's Hill and pounced all over it like a sinister dentist.

Swirl.

The fog did a bit more swirling.

No swirl.

The fog forgot to swirl and just hung around doing nothing.

Swirl, swirl, swirl.

Then it remembered, and went about its business once more. The fog gripped the town in its cold clammy fingers and even the moon was too scared to come out and fight it.

🦗 🦗 🦗

On the high street a single light was shining through the fog. It was coming from the butcher's shop, Billy William the Third's Right Royal Meats. And if you listened carefully, you could just make out the voices coming from within.

'Right, I got a brilliant move,' growled the first voice. 'I'm gonna move me Bishop over there an' smash your Queen up right in her stupid face!'

'Oh, yeah?' rasped the second voice. 'Well, I'm gonna fart all over your Bishop with this one what looks like a little horse!'

And if you had risked a glance through the greasy window you would have seen the owners of those voices, bathed in the flickering light of a candle made from mutton fat. For hunched over the counter were Billy William the butcher, and his filthy pal, Mr Gum. Yes, Mr Gum, with his scraggy red beard and his bloodshot eyes that stared out at you like an octopus curled up in a bad cave. The hideous pair were deep in thought, playing a game of chess as if their stinking lives depended upon it.

But wait! Outside the butcher's shop, something was stirring in the fog. Something large. Something that padded along on all fours. Something that was about to accidentally walk really hard into a lamppost –

GRRFF!

The muffled sound of an animal in pain rang out, but Mr Gum and Billy were so deep in concentration that they didn't even look up at the noise.

Outside in the darkness, the thing dusted itself off. It padded through the fog some more. Then it threw back its big shaggy head, and suddenly the night was filled with a blood-curdling

HA-ROoooOOOOooOOOOOWWWWWLLLL!

All over Lamonic Bibber the townsfolk trembled to hear that roar. And a little boy called Bradley did such a bad mess in his pyjamas that they had to be given to the charity shop the very next day.

HA-ROooooOOOOoOOOoOOOWWWWWLLLL!

'Help! Look out!' cried little Bradley. 'There's a beast on the loose in Lamonic Bibber!'

And with that he ran downstairs, hopped into his father's car and drove to South America where he became a mighty priest. And in all his llong days ruling over the llamas of that lland, Bradley never once spoke of Lamonic Bibber and what he had glimpsed in the fog that night.

Chapter 2
The Next Morning

'NOOOOOOOOOOOOOO!'

The unhappy cry echoed through the early morning air, bringing people running from all over town. And there, still attached to the exclamation mark at the end of the 'NOOOOOOOOOOOOOO!' which was coming from her mouth, they found –

'Old Granny!' exclaimed Jonathan Ripples, the fattest man in town. 'What is it?'

But Old Granny hardly noticed Jonathan Ripples, even though he was about the size of a small circus tent. She was gazing with horror at her garden. Her ancient rose bushes from before the War had been trampled into the mud. And her secret supply of sherry had been emptied into the ornamental bird bath.

'Who did this?' Old Granny asked the starlings who were playing in the bath – but they were far too drunk to tell her. One of them had a little party hat on.

And the destruction didn't stop there. All over town, gardens had been ruined. Small trees had been uprooted, dustbins had been overturned and a garden gnome called Fishin' Tony had died of a heart attack. It was horrible.

'My lawn is torn and now I'm forlorn!' wailed Beany McLeany, who loved things that rhymed.

'My shiny new bike!' sobbed a little girl called Peter. 'I left it outdoors and now look – it's been smashed into six pieces! No, hold on – eight pieces! No, hold on – fourteen!'

'My expensive hedge!' wept David Casserole, the town mayor. 'Nothing's happened to it at all! But imagine if it had, that would have been awful!'

'No, hold on – twenty-three pieces!' sobbed the little girl called Peter.

Yes, the whole town of Lamonic Bibber was in a terrible state. It seemed that everyone had a sad tale to tell, from the tiny baby whose pram had been covered in spit, to the dozens of tramps who'd been pushed into the duck pond while they slept peacefully in the gutter.

But after all the crying had been cried and the last teardrop had been teardropped – that's when the questions began:

'Who could have wreaked such terrible havoc and destruction?'

'Who would even dream of doing such a thing to our little town?'

'Is "teardropped" even a real word?'

At last one man stepped forward with the answers. It was Martin Launderette, who ran the launderette.

'Firstly, I saw who did this thing to our

town,' he said. 'Secondly, "teardropped" isn't a real word at all. And thirdly, it was no human who did this deed. It was a hound. And not just any hound – but a gigantic great tangler of a bark-monster. I saw him last night with my very own eyes that I've known and trusted for years.'

'Martin, just how big was this dog that you supposedly saw?' asked Jonathan Ripples.

'About as big,' whispered Martin dramatically, 'about as big as that dog over there.' And he pointed across the street to where a massive whopper of a dog played happily with an old chip packet, his long golden fur waving merrily in the breeze.

'Now hang on, Mr Laund'rettes,' said a little girl called Polly, who is one of the heroes of this story even though she's only nine. 'Jake's the friendliest, happiest woofdog what ever done bounced through the streets of this town! You better not be accusin' him of all this!'

'I'm not accusing anyone,' muttered Martin Launderette. 'I'm just saying Jake's ruined people's gardens before, that's all. And anyway, who do you think left *this* everywhere?'

He pointed to the clumps of golden fur that lay scattered on the ground. The pieces of little Peter's bicycle were covered with the stuff.

'That fur could be there for a million innocent reasons,' replied Polly indignantly.

'For instances, maybe it fell off a fur tree. An' you oughtn'ts to go whippin' up hatreds towards big friendly dogs without no proofs!'

'Well, there was *something* out there last night,' said Martin Launderette, his eyes darting madly from face to face in the crowd. 'What if it comes back?'

'It's true,' quaked Old Granny, who had been lapping sherry from her bird bath all the while.

'It's true,' shivered the tramps in the duck pond. 'What if it comes back?'

'Well, now,' said Jonathan Ripples, stepping forward boldly, his chins vibrating in the breeze. 'If it comes back it shall have me to contend with. Because yes! I shall guard the town tonight. And if there IS a hound out there, I'll sit on him until he's nothing but a dog-flavoured pancake!'

Chapter 3

Back at the Butcher's Shop

'Look at 'em all,' laughed Mr Gum, as he watched the crowd from Billy William the Third's Right Royal Meats. 'Jumpin' to conclusions like that! What a bunch of ignorant grapes!'

'Ha ha ha,' laughed Billy William, mopping up some pig's blood from the floor with his tongue. 'Ha ha ha.'

'Ha ha ha,' laughed Mr Gum.

'Ho ho ho,' laughed Billy. 'It's funty!'

'Yeah,' agreed Mr Gum. 'It's very "funty" indeed.'

'Another "game of chess" tonight then?' suggested Billy.

'That's right, Billy me boy,' nodded Mr Gum, sucking a lump of rotten pâté from his scruffy red beard. 'Another "game of chess" it is. Ha ha ha ha ha!'

Chapter 4

A Bit More Terror in the Fog

Swirl. Swirl. Swirl.

That night the fog returned. It didn't even bother to phone ahead and check it was OK to come over. It just strolled into town as it pleased, flapping all over the place like an unwelcome ostrich on a train.

Once again, most of the shops on the high street stood dark and silent. Once again, a single light was shining in the butcher's shop. And once again, I'm about to say 'once again'. Because once again, anyone glancing through the greasy window could have seen 'em – those two filthmongers, Mr Gum and Billy William, hunched over the counter at their chessboard.

'Right, I got a brilliant move,' growled Mr Gum. 'I'm gonna move me Bishop over there an' smash your Queen up right in her stupid face!'

'Oh, yeah?' rasped Billy. 'Well, I'm gonna fart all over your Bishop with this one what looks like a little horse!'

♘ ♘ ♘

'What on earth am I doing out here?' trembled Jonathan Ripples as he patrolled the dark streets with only a broken torch and a double cheeseburger for company. He wished he hadn't volunteered to guard the town. What a stupid idea that had been!

He held up the cheeseburger, flapping it open and shut in his chubby hand like a puppet.

'Don't worry,' said Jonathan Ripples in a funny little voice, as if it were the cheeseburger talking. 'Everything's going to be aaaaaall-right.'

'Oh, Burger Boy!' said Jonathan Ripples gratefully. 'Do you really think so?'

'Yes,' squeaked Burger Boy. 'Everything's going to be just –'

HA-ROoooOOOOOOOOOOWWWWWLLLL!

The savage noise cut through the night air like an aeroplane made of teeth.

'Uh-oh,' said Burger Boy.

HA-ROoooOOOOOOOOOOWWWWWLLLL!

'I think it's the Hound,' said Burger Boy. 'Try and stay calm –'

'THE HOUND!' yelped Jonathan Ripples, taking off down the road, Burger Boy clutched tightly in his hand. He tried to run but everything had turned to slow motion, like in a scary film or when your mum goes shopping and drags you round about ten million different shops trying to save twenty pence on a new kettle.

HA-ROoooOOOOOOOOOOOWWWWWLLLL!

'THE HOOOOOUUUND!' screamed Jonathan Ripples – but then he tripped and hit his head hard against the cobblestones. And he was out like a fat light.

Chapter 5

The Townsfolk Point Their Townsfingers

It was Martin Launderette who discovered Jonathan Ripples lying in the road the next morning, covered in fur, dribble and cheeseburger crumbs.

'Martin?' groaned Jonathan Ripples, holding his aching head. 'What happened? And why are there three of you? And where's Burger Boy?'

'I'll tell you what happened!' snorted Martin Launderette, as a crowd gathered to see what was going on. 'The Hound came back, that's what happened! And there he is now!' he yelled, pointing to where Jake the dog was frolicking happily with a sparrow not twenty yards away. 'HE's the one that's been terrorising Lamonic Bibber! – Jake, I mean, not the sparrow,' he added.

The townsfolk looked from the fur on Jonathan Ripples' jumper to the fur on Jake's back. They looked from the dribble on Jonathan Ripples' leg to the drool slurping out of Jake's mouth. Could it be true? Could Jake be behind the whole thing?

'Look at his eyes,' whispered Old Granny, taking a sip of sherry to calm her nerves. 'They're the eyes of an animal!'

'Sometimes good dogs turn naughty,' whispered the little girl called Peter. 'It's true, I saw a documentary about it called *Mummy, Why Did Rover Eat Grandpa?*'

'Is Jake really the dog in the fog and the smog?' whispered Beany McLeany.

'Of course he is!' spat Martin Launderette. 'It's obvious!'

'No, it isn't!' cried Polly. 'It isn't obvious even slightly at all! Has you all got "OUT OF ORDER" signs on your brains?'

But no one paid Polly any heed.

'Jake the dog is a criminal!' shouted Martin Launderette. 'First he attacks our gardens, then he attacks Jonathan Ripples in the fog and murders Burger Boy – where will it all end? We have to get rid of him! Let's send him to Australia on the next boat!'

'Martin Launderette is right!' cried Old Granny, drunkenly waving her bottle of sherry.

'Australia's where he belongs, with all those other naughty dogs!' shouted the little girl called Peter – and soon they were all at it, shouting at poor Jake and poking their tongues out at him and trying to make daddy-long-legses go near him to frighten him.

'What in the name of marmalade's happened to you lot?' cried Polly. 'Sure as squirrels is squirrels, I gots to do somethin' 'bout this!'

Chapter 6

The Greatest
Detective of Them All

Later that morning, a wonderful old fellow called Friday O'Leary was sitting alone in his secret cottage in the woods. He was watching a film on TV about a man sitting alone in a secret cottage in the woods who was watching a film on TV about a man sitting alone in a secret cottage in the woods who was watching a film on TV about a man sitting alone in a secret cottage in the woods who was watching a –

Suddenly – KNOCK! KNOCK! – the doorbell rang.

'Thank goodness,' said Friday,

jumping up from his armchair. 'That film was starting to drive me crazy.'

He threw open the door and there was Polly, standing on the doorstep with a look in her eye that meant business and a hairclip in her hair that meant she'd recently bought a new hairclip.

'Polly!' smiled Friday. 'What brings you all the way out here, little miss?'

'Oh, Frides,' sighed Polly, 'I hardly knows how to begin.'

'Begin at the beginning,' said Friday wisely, tapping his nose. 'And when you get to a bit you can't remember, just make it up.

25

That's what I do.'

☐ ☐ ☐

So Polly told Friday all about it. How the townsfolk were blaming Jake for the night-time attacks, even though they had no proof – and how they were going to send him off to Australia for the crime.

'So who's really behind it, if it's not Jake?' said Friday when Polly had finished. 'It's a mystery. But luckily you've come to the right place. When it comes to solving amazing mysteries, I am the greatest detective of them all.'

'Are you sure?' said Polly.

'Oh, yes,' said Friday, twirling his imaginary detective's moustache grandly. 'Just listen to this and you'll know it must be a fact!'

And slipping on a pair of tap-dancing shoes, he burst into flame. I mean, he burst into song:

I'M A DETECTIVE
*You know I'm not a florist or
a cowboy on the farm
I'm not a lizard keeper at the zoo
I am no baby with a dummy
Always crying for his mummy
So if you ever ask me what I do . . .*

27

CHORUS:
I'm a detective!
I find the clues!
I find the things that others overlook
And I write them down in my little black book
And then I say 'I've solved the crime'
And everyone says 'hooray!'

It's true I'm not a preacher or a teacher
Or a smeacher
You'll never find me cleaning out the drains
I don't work at a factory
That would not be satisfactory
Instead, I use my cunning and
my brains . . .

CHORUS:
I'm a detective!
I've got a hat!
The clues that criminals drop
I tend to spot
And I think about things an awful lot
And then I say, 'I've solved the crime!'
And everyone says 'hooray!'
Yes, everyone says 'hooray!'

Yes, everyone says, 'hooray for Friday!
He's the funkiest, unbelievab'list
Most spectacular, chasing bad
guys-est, Sherlock Holmes-iest,
clue-discov'ring-est
Detective bloke we've ever, EVER
seeeeeeeeen!'

'Well, now do you believe me?' panted Friday.

'I thinks so,' said Polly.

'THE TRUTH IS A LEMON MERINGUE!' yelled Friday, as he sometimes liked to do. 'Let's get detecting!'

Chapter 7

A Clue or Two

*B*ack at Billy William's butcher's shop, Mr Gum and Billy were having a deep and meaningful discussion about life.

'I'll tell you who I hate,' said Mr Gum thoughtfully, as he chewed on an out-of-date pork chop, 'everyone in the world, includin' meself.'

'An' I'll tell you what annoys me,' said Billy, snorting a bunch of entrails up his nose, 'absolutely everythin'.'

'An' I'll tell you what I can't stand,' said Mr Gum. 'Runnin' out of beer. Go an' steal us a few more cans, Billy, me old candlestick.'

'Righty-o,' said Billy.

'An' be quick,' Mr Gum shouted after

him. 'I ain't got all day. Shabba me whiskers!' he muttered. 'It's hard work bein' me. I'd better have a nap.'

And he lay down on the filthy counter, shut his eyes and fell into a half-drunken doze.

RAP! RAP! RAP!

'Eh?' said Mr Gum, starting awake. 'What's that?'

'We knows you're in there, Mr Gum!' yelled a voice. 'Let us in!'

Muttering to himself, Mr Gum unlocked the door. 'Jibbers!' he scowled when he saw Polly and Friday O'Leary standing there on the pavement. 'What do you two meddlers want?'

'Mr Gum, we want to ask you some

questions,' said Friday. 'Questions about the mysterious Hound that's been hounding this town like some sort of hound.'

'Why would I know anythin' about that?' growled Mr Gum, scratching furiously at his dirty red beard.

'Cos you are the worst, Mr Gum,' said Polly. 'Whenever bad stuff happens 'round here you're usually behinds it, or at least standin' quite near it. Now, tell us what you been up to last night when that Hound-dog done attacked Mr Ripples – an' don't you do no lies on me, you rascal de la splarscal!'

'Why,' said Mr Gum, 'I been stayin' 'round here at Billy's. We been playin' chess, that's all. See?' And he pointed to a grimy chessboard which sat on the shop counter.

'Hmm,' said Friday. 'Mind if we take a look?'

'Do what you like, you weirdoes,' scowled Mr Gum. 'See if I care.'

Friday and Polly stepped nervously through the door. It was horrible in there. Bones and bits of meat littered the floor. The walls were crawling with mould. And everywhere you looked there were flies, buzzing through the air or feasting on the slop buckets Billy left out for them. Billy William loved those flies and he knew all their names, even the babies. They were like a family to him.

'Where is Billy, anyway?' asked Friday, brushing a bluebottle called Ian from his hair.

'Billy had to nip out to stea– I mean, to buy some beer,' growled Mr Gum, 'not that it's any of your business, Captain Nosey.'

'Well, who's that then?' said Polly, pointing to a figure lying sprawled on the floor. 'It looks like Billy to me.'

'Borklers!' Mr Gum swore under his breath. 'Oh, yeah, there he is. He must've come back while I was asleep.'

Friday nudged Billy's arm with the toe of his boot. 'Is he all right? He's not moving.'

'He's FINE,' snapped Mr Gum. 'He prob'ly just had too much to drink. Now, forget about Billy, you wanna see this chessboard or not?'

Polly ran her finger over the wooden chessboard and shuddered. The thing was slippery with grease and entrails.

'See?' said Mr Gum triumphantly. 'Me

an' Billy loves our chess. An' if that's a crime then I dunno what this town's comin' to.'

$$\text{\textipa{♟}} \quad \text{\textipa{♟}} \quad \text{\textipa{♟}}$$

'Well, they're def'nitely up to somethin',' exclaimed Polly when they were back outside. 'Did you notice how nervous Mr Gum looked when we was doin' our 'mazin' detectiver stuff?'

'Oh, yes,' lied Friday, 'definitely.'

'An' look,' said Polly, holding up her finger. It was covered with grease from the chessboard. But there was something else there too.

'Fur,' said Friday, screwing his eyes up like he'd once seen a cool detective do on TV. 'Just like the fur when the Hound attacked.'

'Them two's up to somethin',' said

Polly. 'But what we gonna do 'bout it, Frides?'

Friday thought for a moment. Then he thought for another moment. Then he thought for an hour and a half. 'We're going to drink coffee,' he said finally. 'Lots and lots of coffee. Except for you, Polly, you're only nine. You can just look at a photo of some coffee instead.'

'But why, Frides, why?'

'Simple, little miss,' replied Friday, twirling his imaginary detective's moustache so hard it nearly became real for a moment. 'We need to stay awake, because tonight we're going on a stake-out. Plus I quite fancy a coffee anyway.'

Chapter 8
The Stake-out

Swirl.

Night time once again and the fog was back, thick and whirling. Almost everyone in town was fast asleep in bed. Not the same bed, that would be weird. Different beds. In the zoo, all the animals had been switched off for the night. A copy of that morning's *Lamonical Chronicle* blew along the deserted pavement, its headline plain to see:

'JAKE THE DOG MUST GO!' SAY TOWNSFOLK
'I'll kick him out if it's the first thing I do!' vows Martin Lauderette

'Stupid newspaper!' said Polly. She and Friday were crouched down behind a couple of dustbins on the high street, directly opposite the butcher's shop. That way they could lie in wait for the Hound and keep an eye on Mr Gum and Billy at the same time.

'Look,' whispered Polly as the night sky began to cloud over and a damp chill crept into the air, 'it's gonna be another right old fogger-me-smogger.'

'Good,' replied Friday, who had disguised himself as an owl by drawing circles around his eyes and sticking a squeaky toy mouse in his mouth. 'That's exactly what we want. If it's foggy then the Hound – if it really is a hound – will come out. And then we can catch it in our net – if it really is a net.'

🐞 🐞 🐞

'Are stake-outs always this borin'?' said Polly two hours later.

'*SQUEEK*,' replied Friday, chewing on the toy mouse. 'It depends. Generally, in my experience –'

'Hold on,' whispered Polly. 'Somethin's happenin'.'

It was true. Up until that moment the butcher's shop had been completely dark. But now a candle had been lit, its flickering flame just visible through the thick fog.

'*SQUEEK*,' said Friday. 'Let's go and take a closer look.' Friday crept out from behind the dustbin and went slithering across the street on his stomach, keeping his eyes shut so he'd be invisible.

And now they could see Mr Gum and Billy through the shop window. The two of them were hunched over the chessboard, Billy looking thoughtful with one hand to his chin, Mr Gum dangling his Bishop over the board, as if deciding exactly where to place it.

'Right, I got a brilliant move,' they heard Mr Gum growl. 'I'm gonna move me Bishop over there an' smash your Queen up right in her stupid face!'

'*SQUEEK*,' said Friday. 'They really are playing chess!'

'Yeah,' said Polly, 'but I reckons they're jus' fakin' it in case anyone's watchin' them. Any moment now they're gonna stop pretendin', sneak out the door an' go runnin' all over town destroyin' stuff up.'

'You mean –' began Friday.

'Yes,' whispered Polly, 'I reckons Martin Launderette only *thinks* he saw a Hound the other night. If you asks me, what he actually done saw was Mr Gum an' Billy disguised as –'

But at that moment a dreadful howl shattered the silence of the fog, a howl so terrifying that it would have reduced the most courageous eagle on earth to little more than a whimpering doughnut with a beak.

HA-ROoooooooOOOOOOWWWwWLLLL!

'It's the Hound!' chuckled Friday.

'I mean – it's the Hound!' he screamed in terror.

'I don't understands,' said Polly, glancing back at the butcher's, where Mr Gum and Billy were still hunched over their game. 'I was so sure them two was behind it . . .'

HA-RoooooooOOOOOOWWWwWLLLL!

'It seems you were mistaken, little miss,' said Friday. 'There really is a real Hound who's really on the loose for real! Now come on, Polly – after it!' he cried, taking off around the corner, his coat-tails flying out behind him. 'THE TRUTH IS A LEMON MERINGUE!'

'Frides! Frides!' Polly ran after her friend but it was no good – she was instantly lost in the swirling fog.

Swirl, swirl, swirl.

Polly ran up and down the damp cobblestones, the fog closing in all around her. Which way was which? What was what? She didn't have a clue what was going on. It was like being trapped inside a giant French exam.

HA-ROOOOOOOOOOOOOWWWWWLLLL!

The sound seemed to come from right behind her.

HA-ROOOOOOOOOOOOOWWWWWLLLL!

Now it seemed to come from far away.

HA-ROOOOOOOOOOOOOWWWWWLLLL!

Was it to her left?

HA-ROOOOOOOOOOOOOOWWWWWLLLL!

Or her right?

'SQUEEK SQUEEK'

'Frides, is that you?' shouted Polly.

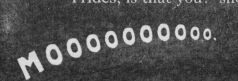
MOOOOOOOOOOO.

What now? Was there a cow loose as well? It was impossible to tell what was happening. Visions of terrible snapping jaws filled Polly's mind, each tooth as sharp as those little spiky bits you get on pineapples . . . Eyes, red in the darkness, red – the colour of blood, the colour of danger, the colour of red things . . .

She felt something huge and heavy and furry land on her back.

A paw! she had time to think – and suddenly the fog wasn't just all around her, it seemed to actually be inside her mind, and the whole world went grey, and she was spinning, spinning towards the cobblestones . . .

Chapter 9

It Was All Just a Bad Dream

When Polly awoke she was back in her cosy pink bed, safe and sound.

'Oh, Mummy,' she exclaimed. 'What a terrible dream I just had! I was running through the fog and there was a horrid great doggie chasing me and –'

'There, there,' said Polly's mother kindly. 'It was only a bad dream. And today is your birthday, remember? Look what we've bought you.'

'Oh, Mummy!' exclaimed Polly, clapping her hands together. 'A new pony and an enormous castle made of chocolate!'

But unfortunately that wasn't the Polly in this story. That was a different Polly who lived in a mansion in New York City, miles and miles away from the little town of Lamonic Bibber.

'La la la la la,' sang the Polly who wasn't in this story. 'I've never once been in danger in my whole life. I'm the luckiest little girl in the world!'

Chapter 10

It Wasn't All Just a Bad Dream

When the Polly in *this* story awoke it was still dark. She was lying outside in the cold and the fog, at the bottom of Boaster's Hill. And the Hound was right there with her, staring directly into her eyes.

'YOIFLE!' screamed Polly. And she fainted all over again.

🐾 🐾 🐾

It was some time later when Polly came to her senses. Through the thinning fog she could see the moon, gazing down upon her with its lonely silver smile, gazing down as if to offer comfort, gazing down as if to say, 'Look out, Polly. Something's licking your knee.'

And it was true. A tongue, rough and wet, was licking her knee. The Hound was licking her knee!

'YOIF–' she began. But then the fog cleared some more and she saw that it was none other than –

'Jake!' exclaimed Polly. 'But if you're out here in the middle of the night . . . I dunno what to think. Is it you what's the Hound after all? Say it isn't true, even though you can't do no words!'

HA-ROOOOOOOOOOOOOWWWWWLLLL!

The now familiar howl came then from the other side of town. It was followed by a distant cry –

'SQUEEK. SQUEEK. SQUEEK.
THE TRUTH IS A LEMON MERINGUE!'

'So hang on,' said Polly slowly.
'Friday's still out there right now, chasin'
the real Hound. An' that means you CAN'T
be the Hound, Jakey! You're innocent! Oh,
I knowed it!'

'BARK BARK BARK,' said Jake,
licking Polly's eyebrows happily and
making her laugh despite it all.

And Polly buried her face in the
big dog's side and cried tears of relief
and misery and happiness all rolled up
into a brand new super-emotion called
'remippiness'. And there she stayed, safe
and warm until morning, stroking Jake's
soft golden fur and feeling him breathe in
and out like the good dog he truly was.

Chapter 11

The Singing Detective

'What do we do now, Frides?' said Polly as they wandered the streets of the town, Jake at their side. 'We knows Jakey's innocent as a newborn baby peanut. But how we gonna proof it?'

Friday's imaginary moustache drooped sadly. He had been up all night chasing the Hound and he was cold and hungry and tired. And not only that, but his toy mouse had been eaten by a toy cat when he wasn't looking.

'Let's get some breakfast,' he said, 'that ought to cheer us up.'

But every café on the high street had the same sign in the window:

NO DOGS ALLOWED
APART FROM ONES THAT
AREN'T JAKE

And every face they passed on the rainy streets that morning told the same story of fear, resentment and not liking Jake very much.

'That dog's a menace,' trembled Old Granny, who had been drinking sherry all morning to calm her nerves. 'I'll be glad when he's gone!'

'Your big wet pet makes me very upset,' rhymed Beany McLeany.

'I don't like him either, even though I don't really know what's going on,' said a passing American tourist.

'Uh-oh,' said Polly as they approached the launderette, where a large crowd had gathered. 'This looks like troubles.'

And it was troubles. An enormous washing machine stood upon the pavement and standing on the washing machine, jiggling crazily up and down as it spun, was Martin Launderette.

'LOOK!' he yelled when he saw Jake approaching. 'There he is! He's not a dog! He's a devil in disguise! As a dog!'

'WOOF!' said Jake, rolling over on to his back, hoping for a friendly tickle.

'Have you ever seen such a terrifying beast?' spat Martin Launderette. 'But never fear, townsfolk. The boat to Australia leaves at nine o'clock tomorrow morning! And I'll personally ensure that dog's on it!'

'Hooray for Martin Launderette!' shouted the crowd. 'Hooray for Martin L!'

🎲 🎲 🎲

'Oh, Frides,' said Polly as they walked away, the cheers of the crowd still ringing in their ears. 'We gots one more night to proof Jake's innocences, or it's off to 'Stralia for him an' that's the last we'll ever see of his lovely paws. What we gonna do?'

'Um, I could sing "I'm A Detective" again,' suggested Friday.

'I don't supposes it will help much, Frides,' said Polly sadly. 'But go on, I knows how you loves your sing-songery.'

'OK,' said Friday, slipping into his tap-dancing shoes. 'Here goes!

I'M A DETECTIVE

*You know I'm not a florist or a
cowboy on the farm
I'm not a lizard keeper at the zoo
I am no baby with a dummy
Always crying for his mummy
So if you ever –*

– why, Polly, what on earth's the matter?'

But Polly barely heard him. She was frozen to the spot, her hand paused in mid-stroke through Jake's spongy tongue.

'What's wrong, little miss?' asked Friday again.

'I . . . It's . . . It's all . . . makin' senses,' whispered Polly. 'It's all comin' together.' All the hairs on her head were standing on end. Her arms were covered in goosebumps. It felt like someone had poured special **Detective Sauce**™ into her head and was cooking her brains in a

'Frides,' said Polly slowly, 'can you sing that last bit again?'

'I am no baby with a dummy. Always crying for his mummy –' sang Friday – and that was it. The final piece of the puzzle slotted into place and Polly's brain went 'DING!' so loudly even Friday heard it.

'HOFFLESTICKS!' she exclaimed. 'Now I knows how them villains was able to get 'way with it, the sneakies! Come on, Frides,' said Polly. 'You're gonna need loads more coffee to keeps you awake. An' I'm a-gonna needs to look at a photo of the strongest cup of coffee what's ever been brewed. We gotta do another stake-out – an' we gotta do it tonights!'

Chapter 12

The Hound of Lamonic Bibber

Swirl.

The final night – and the fog had returned. Polly and Friday crouched outside the butcher's shop, hardly daring to breathe in case somebody heard them, but hardly daring not to breathe in case they died from not breathing. It was a difficult one.

Swirl. swirl. swirl.

Thicker than ever, the fog crept secretively through the town, wrapping itself around lampposts and dustbins like a ghost, turning everything it touched into a mystery.

"Tis the worst fog this town has ever

seen,' whispered Old Granny. ''Tis the worst –'

'Go back home, Old Granny,' whispered Friday kindly. 'You're not meant to be in this bit of the story.'

'Sorry,' said Old Granny, who was a bit drunk. Taking a sip of sherry from the bottle she always kept hidden in the fog she toddled off home, leaving Polly and Friday to get on with their stake-out.

It was all down to them now. If they'd guessed right, Jake's name would be cleared forever and he'd be welcomed back to run and romp and roll through the streets of the town like always.

But if they'd guessed wrong? Well, then. That was the end for old Jakey boy. He'd be carted off to Australia like a sack of wizards, and Polly would never see him again, except in her tears. Perhaps, she thought, other children would one day play with him and ride upon his back for their fun. Other children who were unaware that he'd once been called Jake. They'd probably name him 'Stuart' or 'Bouncyface' or "Sydney Opera Dog'. It didn't bear thinking about.

🦀 🦀 🦀

'Not much longer now,' whispered Polly, her teeth chattering against the cold. And even as she spoke, a candle was lit inside the butcher's shop. Polly risked a glance through the window and saw the two men in their usual positions, hunched over their game of chess.

'OK,' said Friday. 'They're ready. Let's go.'

The detectives crept around the side of the butcher's shop and tiptoed up the fire escape. Bodies flat against the tarmac roof, they peered down upon the stinking bins and rubbish that littered the alleyway below.

For a few minutes more they lay there in silence. It seemed like nothing was going to happen.

Swirl, swirl, swirl.

The fog enshrouded them, tugging at their sleeves, whispering like a dead man into their ears.

Then . . .

Creeeeaaaaaaak . . .

The back door to the shop creaked softly open.

Shuffle, shuffle, shuffle.

A large bulky shape padded out into

the misty alleyway.

It was the beast that had terrorised the town for over ten chapters!

It was the monster that haunted everyone's darkest dreams!

It was the Hound of Lamonic Bibber!

HA-ROoooOOOoOOOOOWWWWWLLLL!

Even though Polly knew better, a shiver ran up her spine. What if she was wrong? What if she was messing with forces she didn't understand? The fog swirled all around, striking fear into her heart and fog into her nostrils, and for just one moment Polly was tempted to drive to South America, become a priest and forget about the whole thing.

'But no,' she whispered to herself through clenched teeth. 'I've come too far to give up like a pathetic cornflake! Come on, Frides! RELEASE THE NET!'

And that was the secret signal for Friday to release the net.

HA-ROOO?

The Hound looked up.

The net came down.

The Hound's bloodshot eyes flashed furiously.

HA-ROOOOOOOOOOOOOOWWWWLLLL!

But it was no good howling at the net. The net wasn't scared. It was a net.

GRRR!! SNRURURHSH! MMMMMMMFFFFF!

The Hound staggered like a mad thing around the alleyway, overturning bins of rotten meat, clumps of fur flying everywhere.

But the more it tried to tear itself free, the more it clawed and pawed and roared, the more entangled it became. Until eventually it gave up and collapsed in a filthy heap, breathing in great ragged gasps, huge green flies buzzing all around it like dirty spaceships circling a horrible new planet called Stenchulos 9.

Cautiously the detectives climbed down from the roof and approached their hideous catch.

'Look,' whispered Polly, training her torch-beam upon the humped-up shape. 'There can't be no doubt 'bout it. This is the naughty shambler what's been doin' all them bads.'

Yes, it was true. The Hound's hide was covered with stains and stinks from its night-time adventures. Its fur was streaked with grass and mud, it reeked of Old Granny's sherry – and the handlebars of little Peter's bicycle were still stuck to one of its legs.

'So there really was a Hound after all,' nodded Friday wisely. 'Just as I thought.'

'But wait, Frides.' Polly was down on her hands and knees in the filthy alleyway as she pulled away the heavy net. Screwing her face up with bravery and facial muscles, she dug both hands deep into the Hound's shaggy fur and flung it aside to reveal . . .

Well, that's all we've got time for, folks. I'm afraid we've run out of pages. We hope you have enjoyed this special World Book Day presentation. Look out for all the other great World Book Day titles, including The Spook's Tale *by Joseph Delaney;* Ten Stations *by Jenny Valentine; and* Cobbler Versus the Mango Bandits *by Mimsy Rogers, and remember, kids – a good book is like a friend who's made of paper.*

What's that?

We do have time?

Oh, marvellous. Let's get back to the story then . . .

'So there really was a Hound after all,' nodded Friday wisely. 'Just as I thought.'

'But wait, Frides.' Polly was down on her hands and knees in the filthy alleyway as she pulled away the heavy net. Screwing her face up with bravery and facial muscles, she dug both hands deep into the Hound's shaggy fur and flung it aside to reveal . . .

'Woof,' scowled Mr Gum, his bloodshot eyes blazing like lanterns.

'Woof, woof,' said Billy William, his arms wrapped tight around Mr Gum's waist. A tail made from rope hung limply from the back of Billy's apron. 'Bark, bark, bark.'

'It's no good tryin' to fool us no more, you bad men,' said Polly. 'We seen through your ratty old disguises. An' it looks like it's checkmate for you!'

Chapter 13

And Everyone Says 'Hooray!'

'So you see,' Polly told the crowd outside the butcher's shop later that morning, 'it was Mr Gum an' Billy all along. Every night they done dressed up in their stinky old fur coat an' terrorised the town.'

'But I saw them playing chess the night the Hound attacked me and Burger Boy,' frowned Jonathan Ripples. 'How could they be in two places at once?'

'I wondered 'bout that myself, Mr Ripples, sir,' said Polly. 'My suspicions was first 'roused when I saw Billy William a-lyin' on the butcher's shop floor. He didn't look quite right an' he wasn't movin' one tiny bit. An' then Friday's brilliant song done gave me the important clue what I needed to work it out.'

I am no baby with a dummy

sang Friday, slipping into his tap-dancing shoes once more.

'An' it was that word – "dummy" – what done it,' said Polly, leading the amazed crowd into the butcher's shop where Mr Gum and Billy still sat hunched over their chessboard.

'Splib!' trembled Old Granny. 'Watch out, Polly!'

'Don't worry,' said Polly, tugging at Mr Gum's beard only to have it come off in her hand. 'See? They isn't nothin' but plastic shop dummies. Dummies. Jus' like Friday said in his song. The real culprits are tied up 'gainst the Oak Tree of Shame in the town square.'

'The villains also used this to aid in their ingenious illusion,' continued Friday, reaching below the counter and producing a battered old tape recorder covered in grease. 'Observe,' he said, pressing PLAY.

'Right, I got a brilliant move,' growled Mr Gum's voice from the machine. 'I'm gonna move me Bishop over there –'

But Friday had pressed STOP. He could stand to hear the villains' voices no more, and also he just enjoyed pressing buttons.

'So it was just Mr Gum and Billy up to their usual mischief,' said David Casserole, the town mayor. 'What a terrible scheme, trying to get rid of Jake the dog like that! But you caught them, Friday. You are truly the greatest detective of them all.'

'Thank you, your majesty,' said Friday graciously, 'but I can't accept your speech. It makes me puke deep down inside where the truth really lies. The fact is, there is one greater even than I.'

And so saying, he took out an imaginary detective's razor and shaved off his imaginary detective's moustache.

'Here,' said Friday, handing the moustache to Polly. 'This belongs to you now. Put it on, little miss,' he urged, 'put it on.'

And so, with tears in her eyes, Polly donned that legendary invisible facial hair.

And then she said, 'I've solved the crime!'

And everyone said 'hooray!'

Yes, everyone said 'hooray!'

Chapter 14

Another Case Closed

'Townsfolk, you got some massive 'pologisin' to do,' said Polly, her imaginary moustache fluttering grandly in the breeze. 'You oughtn'ts to go whippin' up hatreds towards big friendly dogs without no proofs – an' that's a Official Polly Bit of Advice.'

'Well said, Polly,' agreed Mayor Casserole. 'We shall engrave your ancient words upon the side of the Town Hall this very day. And Martin Launderette shall be Officially Sat On by Jonathan Ripples until sundown. Now, as for the villains,' he continued, 'they are the ones that must be sent to Australia, to work on the spider farms along with all the other prisoners.'

But when he went to untie the villains from the Oak Tree of Shame, he got a nasty surprise. Billy William's arm came away in his hand and Mr Gum's head rolled off into a flowerbed and ran over a dormouse.

'Oh, MARZIPAN,' sighed Polly. 'It's jus' them shop dummies again. The real villains must've done a crafty swap an' run off down the road, drinkin' beer an' laughin' like rattlesnakes.'

And it was true. That was exactly what had happened, and who knew when next they would return? But as everyone agreed, the important thing was that Jake the dog had been proven innocent and for the rest of that day he was treated like a king and paraded round town in a big golden taxi, barking victoriously for all to hear.

🛡 🛡 🛡

But what of Lamonic Bibber itself? Well, you've never seen such a feast! Even the tramps in the duck pond were allowed a nibble. There was food and laughter and singing and dancing, and then more food and more laughter and more singing and more dancing. And then MORE food and MORE laughter and MORE singing and MORE dancing. And then everyone was sick.

And later still, when the feasting was at an end and all the vomit had been cleared up by trained badgers, Polly and Friday sat together in the town square, gazing up at a clear evening sky in which not a trace of fog could be seen. The moon was out and the twinkling stars danced a waltz in its silvery light.

'Frides,' said Polly at length. 'Whatever anyone says, you'll always be the greatest detectiver in my little eyes. I'm well proud to know you.'

'As well you should be,' said a voice from behind her. And without turning around, Polly knew it was the Spirit of the Rainbow, for she could feel the warmth of his honesty radiating from him like a miniature boy-shaped sun.

'Child,' said the Spirit of the Rainbow to Polly, even though he was no older than she. 'Because of you, the world is once more glowing with happy colours. You have done well, and you shall forever be remembered, not just in your lifetime but for many –'

'Spirit!' called a voice from the other side of the town square. 'It's yer uncle Ken on the phone! Come and talk to him!'

'Oops, gotta go,' said the Spirit of the Rainbow. And he tossed the detectives a couple of fruit chews and off he ran.

'Frides, what do you think the Spirit done meant 'bout bein' remembered forever an' ever?' asked Polly as they watched him go.

'Why, don't you know, little miss?' laughed Friday. 'It means your words and actions are so magnificent that no one will ever forget them. Look,' he said pointing across the square.

For the engravers had finished their work. And there upon the side of the Town Hall, just as Mayor Casserole had commanded, were Polly's words, in letters five feet high:

YOU OUGHTN'TS TO GO
WHIPPIN' UP HATREDS
TOWARDS BIG FRIENDLY DOGS
WITHOUT NO PROOFS!

And as far as I, or anyone else knows, those words are written there still.

THE END

NATIONAL
BOOK
tokens

This book has been specially written
and published for *World Book Day 2009*.

World Book Day is a worldwide
celebration of books and reading,
and was marked in over 30 countries
around the globe last year.

For further information please see
www.worldbookday.com

World Book Day in the UK and Ireland is made possible
by generous sponsorship from National Book Tokens,
participating publishers, authors and booksellers.
Booksellers who accept the £1 World Book Day Token
kindly agree to bear the full cost of redeeming it.

FREE COLLECTOR CARDS INSIDE!

Coming May 2009

Series 4
THE AMULET OF AVANTIA

Tom's Quest to collect the pieces of amulet from the deadly Ghost Beasts is the only way to save his father...

978 1 40830 376 4   978 1 40830 377 1   978 1 40830 378 8

978 1 40830 379 5   978 1 40830 381 8   978 1 40830 380 1

All priced at £4.99

Vedra & Krimon: Twin Beasts of Avantia, *Spiros the Ghost Phoenix* and *Arax the Soul Stealer* are priced at £5.99

Series 3
THE DARK REALM

To rescue the good Beasts, Tom must brave the terrifying Dark Realm and six terrible new Beasts...

TORGOR

978 1 84616 997 7

SKOR

978 1 84616 998 4

NARGA

978 1 40830 000 8

KAYMON

978 1 40830 001 5

TUSK

978 1 40830 002 2

STING

978 1 40830 003 9

SPECIAL BUMPER EDITION!

978 1 40830 382 5

Arax has stolen
Aduro's soul – and
now he wants Tom's...

Series 2
THE GOLDEN ARMOUR

Tom must find the pieces of the magical golden armour.
But they are guarded by six terrifying Beasts!

978 1 84616 988 5   978 1 84616 989 2   978 1 84616 990 8

978 1 84616 991 5   978 1 84616 992 2   978 1 84616 993 9

Will Tom find Spiros
in time to save his
aunt and uncle?

978 1 84616 994 6

Series 1
BEAST QUEST

An evil wizard has enchanted the Beasts that guard
Avantia. Is Tom the hero who can free them?

FERNO
978 1 84616 483 5

SEPRON
978 1 84616 482 8

ARCTA
978 1 84616 484 2

TAGUS
978 1 84616 486 6

NANOOK
978 1 84616 485 9

EPOS
978 1 84616 487 3

SPECIAL BUMPER EDITION!

VIPRA & TRINION
978 1 84616 951 9

Can Tom save the baby
dragons from Malvel's
evil plans?

 ## Can YOU survive
the BEAST QUEST?

Read all of Tom's incredible adventures as he battles
the fearsome Beasts sent by evil Wizard Malvel.
Together with his loyal friend Elenna, his trusty
steed Storm and Silver the grey wolf, Tom risks
everything in his fight for the freedom of Avantia.

Will good conquer evil? Or will Malvel and his
Beasts destroy the kingdom? As long as there is
blood in his veins, Tom is determined to stop him...

Do BATTLE with
your friends!

Each exciting story comes with FREE collector cards!
Cut them out and play with your friends. Keep an
eye out for a special exclusive collector card – check
the Beast Quest website for details.

www.beastquest.co.uk

Fight the Beasts,
Fear the Magic

www.beastquest.co.uk

Check out the Beast Quest website for games, downloads, competitions, animations and all the latest news about Beast Quest. Sign up to the newsletter at www.beastquest.co.uk to receive exclusive extra content and the opportunity to enter special members-only competitions.

Email beastquest@hachettechildrens.co.uk for your exclusive Beast Quest game poster!

Win an exclusive Beast Quest T-shirt and goody bag!

To enter this competition, just answer these two easy questions:
1) Who sent the Book of Worlds to Avantia?
2) In 30 words or fewer, tell us why you love Beast Quest!

Send your entry on a postcard to:

Beast Quest World Book Day Competition
Orchard Books
338 Euston Road
London NW1 3BH

Don't forget to include your name and address.

Ten random prize-winners will be drawn from all correct entries received.
Closing date: 31 May 2009
(Competition open to UK and Eire residents only.)

"Who fired that?" he yelled, bouncing to his feet again.

Elenna ran over, bow in hand, and halted in front of the Captain. "Sorry," she said. "It was one of my cadets. He hasn't quite got the hang of archery yet, I'm afraid."

Tom hid a smile. He knew perfectly well that Elenna had fired the arrow herself. Just because they weren't on a Beast Quest didn't mean that he and Elenna wouldn't watch each other's backs anymore.

A voice called out from the palace gardens. "He has returned! Taladon the Swift has returned!"

Tom froze. *Taladon? My father?*

Follow this Quest to the end in NIXA THE DEATH-BRINGER, Tom's first adventure in Series 4, The Amulet of Avantia.

Tom heard heavy footsteps. Captain Harkman's feet halted beside him; he was tapping his whip against his polished riding boots.

"Slacking again?" Captain Harkman snarled. He crouched down beside Tom, so that Tom could see his red, sweating face and gingery hair. "You're just like your father. He was a slacker, too."

Fury flooded through Tom. He gritted his teeth together with the effort of controlling his temper.

"Taladon trained here once, when he was a young man," the Captain went on, straightening up. "I was glad to see the back of him. He was lazy, and arrogant too. He was—"

Tom heard the sound of an arrow whizzing through the air. It just missed Captain Harkman's head as he ducked and rolled away.

Ask, and it's yours."

"Thank you, sire," Tom replied. "I'd like to be a soldier in your army."

He'd thought it would be fun, and a great way to go on helping Avantia. *But I was wrong*, he sighed to himself. What was the point of doing press-ups all day long when he had powers that the cadet officer, Captain Harkman, could only dream of?

"I made a mistake," Tom muttered to himself as his arms pumped up and down. "I wish there was something else I could do. Maybe another Quest..."

He snatched a glance across the courtyard to where his friend, Elenna, was teaching archery to the youngest cadets. He watched her positioning one boy's fingers on the bowstring, and saw his face break into a delighted grin as his arrow thumped home.

CHAPTER ONE

A FATHER RETURNS

"One hundred and fifty-one! One hundred and fifty-two!" Captain Harkman's voice echoed across the training courtyard.

Tom groaned as he pumped his arms in yet another press-up. He thought he was going to die of boredom, if he didn't first melt into a puddle under the hot sun of Avantia.

He remembered how he had returned from Gorgonia a few weeks before, fresh from the Quest on which he had defeated the evil Wizard Malvel for the third time.

"Avantia owes you a great debt," the King had said. "Tom, you may choose any position you like in my court.

Here's a sneak preview of Tom's next exciting adventure!

Meet

NIXA
THE
DEATH-BRINGER

Only Tom can defeat the Ghost Beasts and save his father...

Avantia needs a hero...

It is written in the Ancient Scripts that the peaceful kingdom of Avantia shall one day be plunged into peril.

Now that time has come.

Malvel the Dark Wizard threatens the land with his evil. His ferocious Beasts terrorise the people and will destroy Avantia if they are not defeated.

But the Ancient Scripts also predict an unlikely hero. It is foretold that a boy will take up the Quest to fight the Beasts and free the kingdom of Malvel...

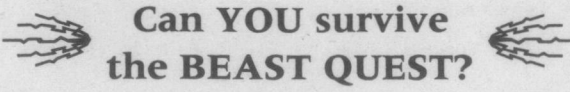

Can YOU survive the BEAST QUEST?

With special thanks to Michael Ford
For Henry Nettleton, brave and true

www.beastquest.co.uk

ORCHARD BOOKS
338 Euston Road, London NW1 3BH
Orchard Books Australia
Level 17/207 Kent St, Sydney, NSW 2000

A Paperback Original
First published in Great Britain in 2009

Beast Quest is a registered trademark of
Working Partners Limited
Series created by Working Partners Limited, London

Text © Working Partners Limited 2009
Cover and inside illustrations by Steve Sims
© Orchard Books 2009

A CIP catalogue record for this book is available
from the British Library.

ISBN 978 0 95594 462 8

1 3 5 7 9 10 8 6 4 2

Printed in the UK by CPI Bookmarque, Croydon, CR0 4TD
Cover repro by Saxon Photolitho, Norwich, Norfolk

The paper and board used in this paperback are natural
recyclable products made from wood grown in sustainable
forests. The manufacturing processes conform to the
environmental regulations of the country of origin.

Orchard Books is a division of Hachette Children's Books,
an Hachette UK company.

www.hachette.co.uk

SephiR
THE
STORM MONSTER

BY ADAM BLADE
INSPIRED BY KIERON CAMERON

ORCHARD BOOKS

*G*reetings, and welcome to the Kingdom of Avantia. I am Aduro, wizard of King Hugo's realm. I come to tell you that a time of great peril is upon us.

Once every generation, a battle must take place, the likes of which your world will never see. The chosen Master of the Beasts has to take on the Dark Wizard, Malvel, for the ultimate prize: the Book of Worlds.

Should the Book fall into evil hands, there is no telling the death and destruction that may entail.

The Master of the Beasts has nothing on his side but courage and the support of his loyal companions. Will that be enough to defeat Malvel's greatest evil yet?

There is only one way of finding out...

Aduro

PROLOGUE

"What is it, boy?" said Simon, Avantia's shepherd. His dog Max's ears were pressed back, and he was looking west towards the mountains.

Over the hills, Simon could see what he thought was a bird. But it was huge!

The shape sailed through the sky, getting closer, as the sheep nervously huddled together.

It became bigger and stretched into a column. As a howling sound screeched in Simon's ears, he finally realised what he was looking at.

A tornado – heading straight for the flock!

Simon looked around desperately for somewhere to hide. A huge oak tree grew at the edge of the meadow. He ran towards it.

"Max!" he shouted. He gave a series of short whistles, and Max darted behind the flock, guiding the sheep towards the sheltering branches.

The noise of the twister had become a roar, and the air was suddenly cold.

Simon could see debris caught in the walls of the tornado, whipped up and spinning in the wind.

Wait. There was something else.

As the column bulged, shapes began to form in the coils of the twister.

Simon could see the hollows of two eyes...the curl of a sneer... It was a face!

The tornado was closing in on him fast. Its mouth gaped open, and a terrible scream filled Simon's ears.

The wind slammed into the oak tree.

Simon felt his body being lifted from the ground. He clutched at the empty air until his fingers closed on something – a

branch! He hung on, the wind whipping his body upwards and wrenching his arms. Beneath him, he could see his sheep being flung across the mountain.

With a final wail, the storm passed. Simon dared to look around him.

The tree had been stripped bare. There was no sign of the flock, other than the odd scrap of white fleece among the debris.

Shaking, Simon clambered to the ground.

"Max!" he called out.

There was no answer.

"Max! Where are you, boy?"

Still nothing. Simon staggered down the hillside. His best friend and his precious herd had gone forever.

He fell to his knees. Whatever was driving that tornado was evil to the core…

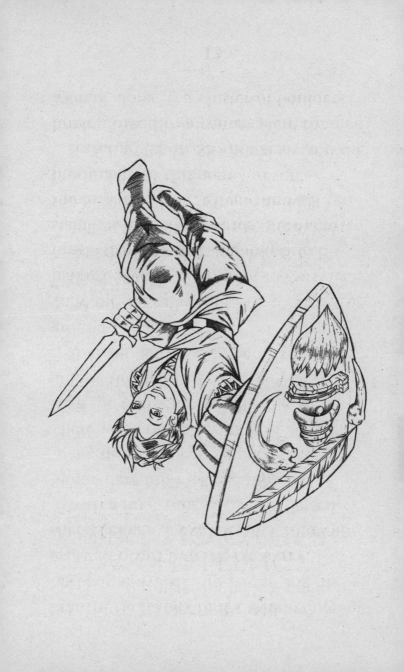

CHAPTER ONE

A CHALLENGE
LIKE NO OTHER

Tom and Elenna were riding across the plains of Avantia. Tom kicked his heels into Storm's jet-black flanks and his stallion charged forwards, his mane rippling in the air. Silver the wolf ran fluidly beside them.

Tom tugged on Storm's reins and the horse slowed to a canter as he climbed a small slope to a cluster of boulders.

13

Silver threaded between the rocks, his pink tongue lolling.

"Look," said Elenna, pointing. "That rock doesn't seem right."

Tom followed the line of her finger, and saw that one of the rocks was vibrating, as though there was an earthquake. But the ground beneath his feet wasn't moving. Silver gave a series of nervous barks.

The boulder suddenly seemed to melt, then changed shape, becoming a tall column.

"Stay back," said Tom to Elenna, pulling his sword from its scabbard.

The shifting rock took on the shape of a body.

"What are you?" he demanded.

A chuckle answered him. "You won't need a sword."

Tom recognised the voice. "Aduro!"

It was the good wizard who'd helped them on their Beast Quests. The rock changed again, becoming the bright cloth of Aduro's robe. Suddenly he was before them, in the flesh.

"I'm sorry to have startled you. I come with an important challenge," said the wizard, his face serious.

"Another Beast Quest?" Tom asked.

"Of a kind," said Aduro. "Let me show you something."

The wizard waved his hand, and the air beside him shimmered. An image appeared. In a snowy wasteland, a great white-haired Beast, with yellow claws and a furry face, was gripping a man in its fist.

"That's Nanook!" cried Elenna, recognising the snow monster they had rescued on an earlier Quest.

The man in the image was brandishing a sword. Suddenly, a dragon swooped into the picture and released a spurt of fire. The man lifted his shield and the flames bounced off the surface. Nanook roared and lifted the man higher still. He sliced with his sword, hacking at the dragon's scales. Then, with another wave of Aduro's hand, the image faded away.

"That was the Battle of the Beasts," the wizard explained, "held once every generation between the forces of good and evil. The Master of the Beasts must fight his arch enemy – and each may choose a Beast to help him. Now, Tom, it is your turn."

"But who is my arch enemy?" asked Tom.

"It has to be Seth," said Elenna. With a dreadful feeling of certainty, Tom knew his friend was right. He nodded. The boy Seth was Malvel's champion and loyal servant. He and Tom had had swordfights almost to the death.

"What's that?" asked Tom, pointing. A shimmering image of a leather-bound book had appeared by Aduro's side. It had gilt edges and a silver lock on the front.

"This," said Aduro, "is the Book

of Worlds, sent to Avantia by Kieron the Great many moons ago. It is what you will be duelling for. Its pages contain many secrets about the kingdom of Avantia and the worlds beyond. It can be used for great good, or great evil. It must never fall into Malvel's hands."

Tom couldn't remember ever seeing an object so beautiful. What secrets were hiding among its pages?

"I won't let you down," he said, his heart brimming with determination.

"It's time for you to select the Beast who will help you in the battle. Choose wisely," said Aduro.

Tom looked at the surface of his shield, where the tokens he had recovered from each of the good Beasts of Avantia were lodged: a fragment of horseshoe from Tagus the horse-man, a tooth from Sepron the sea serpent, a talon from Epos the flame bird, an eagle's feather from Arcta the mountain giant and a bell from Nanook. Each gave him a special power. His eye finally fell on the last token – Ferno's dragon scale.

All the tokens began glowing. As the shield lit up with rainbow colours, Tom saw six silhouettes appear on the horizon. Six Beasts – the first Beasts Tom had ever encountered. They had come to help him. He could see Arcta's

shaggy fur and the snow-white pelt
of Nanook the snow monster. Epos
swooped through the air and Tagus
pawed the ground. Tom laughed with
joy to see them all again.

"Who will you choose?" asked
Elenna, waving at their friends.

"I choose Ferno, fire dragon of the
mountain!" Ferno was the first Beast
Tom had ever come across, and it
would be good to be reunited with
him again.

He held out his shield and it vibrated
on his arm.

Ferno flew up high into the sky,
blotting out the sun, and the air was
filled with an almighty roar of
approval from the Beasts.

The dragon swooped towards them.
His great dark wings beat the air,
powering through the sky. With a toss

of his spiky head, two jets of flame
exploded from his nostrils.

Ferno was coming!

A SUPER-BEAST

"He's magnificent!" gasped Elenna.

"A good choice," said Aduro, smiling. The five remaining Beasts waved and turned away. They would help another day.

Ferno swooped low over the plain. Then he extended his black talons, landing gently on the rocks beside them. The smells of sulphur and soot were heavy in the air.

"Are you ready to face Malvel's evil again?" Tom asked the Beast.

The fire dragon lifted his head and sent out a jet of flames.

"Your bravery will be sorely tested, Tom," said Aduro. "Whatever it takes, Malvel must not get his hands on the Book. The whole of Avantia is relying on you."

Tom climbed along the hard ridges of Ferno's tail, then jumped onto the dragon's back between his wings.

"With Ferno and Elenna at my side," Tom said, "there's no way Seth will capture the Book of Worlds."

The dragon rose to his feet, with Tom holding on tight to his scales. He looked down at Elenna and Aduro. Storm flicked his tail and whinnied, while Silver leapt up and down on the spot.

"Good luck, Tom!" Elenna cried,
waving her hand in farewell. "I'm here
if you need me."

Aduro lifted his hands, and there was a mighty *swoosh*. All around the horizon the sky changed colour, turning a darker shade of blue. It looked like a rainstorm, but the downpour was going upwards, climbing from the ground into the sky.

"What's that?" Tom asked.

"No one from Avantia must see the battle," said Aduro. "This magical rainstorm will shield it from their eyes. Seth will be here soon, and I must be gone. Goodbye, Tom, and good luck!"

Aduro's form folded in on itself. But instead of becoming a rock once more, what remained was a plinth. Resting on top was the Book of Worlds. Tom wondered if he should take the Book now, to keep it safe...

"Are you ready to die, Tom?" shouted a voice.

Seth! Ferno twisted round to face their enemy.

The wicked boy was riding a Beast of his own – a lion with three terrifying heads. It was Trillion, come back to life! The Beast bounded across the plain with Seth on his back. The boy's pale hair reflected the sunlight like marble and his cold blue eyes flashed. When he tugged on the lion's mane, all three sets of jaws opened with a deafening roar, revealing blood-stained teeth that were sharp enough to tear flesh.

Ferno took to the air. He flew low towards Seth and Trillion, his wing tips stroking the grass. Seth didn't move.

Tom smiled to himself. *This will be easier than I thought!*

A hiss split the air like a red-hot sword being plunged into water.

"Tom, look out!" Elenna screamed.

Something hammered into Tom's stomach, throwing him clear of Ferno's back. He slammed into the ground, gasping for breath.

What was that?

A great shadow appeared and Tom rolled out of the way just as a slithering red and green tail thumped

28

the ground. Tom sprang to his feet, and found himself face to face with Vipero the snake man. Where had he come from? Tom had already defeated him once! Vipero's two snake heads hissed through their poisonous fangs. Tom drew his sword as one of the heads darted towards him. The blade glanced off the thick scales, and Vipero slithered back towards Seth and Trillion.

So that's Malvel's game, Tom thought. *Two Beasts against one.*

Ferno landed beside him and Tom leapt onto the dragon's back. A howl echoed across the plain. Now a third Beast was beside Seth and Trillion. Thick brown fur covered its ape-like face, and red bloodshot eyes glared out at him.

Claw.

The giant monkey beat his massive chest with two clawed arms, and the noise was like a drum. He howled again, showing his thick yellow teeth, and leapt into the air. Whatever evil magic Malvel was using, it looked like he was able to bring the evil Beasts of Gorgonia back to life – even after Tom had defeated them.

The three Beasts closed together. Claw climbed onto Vipero's back. Trillion moved in front of Vipero.

Tom blinked. *This can't be happening*, he thought.

The three Beasts were merging. Now there was only a single Beast where three had stood before. All that was left of the giant monkey were his long, bristling arms, ending in his razor-sharp claws. They were attached to the glistening, scaly body of Vipero. But

instead of the snake man's snouts, it was the three heads of Trillion that stared back at Tom.

They let out a roar that vibrated through Tom's chest. Ferno circled the air and Tom saw Elenna place an arrow to her bow and train its point on the Beast's heart. But even from this distance, Tom could see her hand trembling.

Malvel had created a Super-Beast!

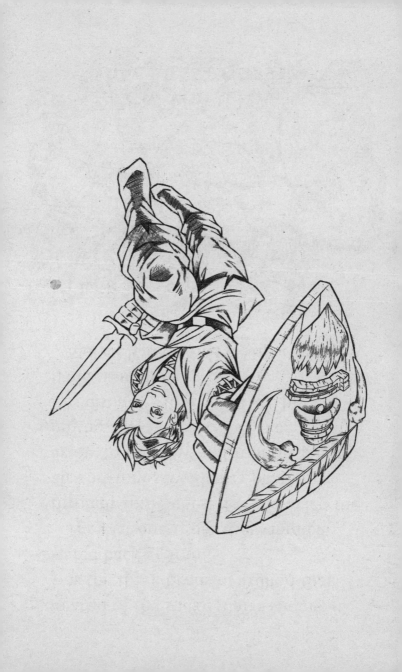

CHAPTER THREE

BENDING
THE RULES

Ferno roared. With a few beats of his powerful wings, he and Tom were above Seth and the Super-Beast, hovering beneath Aduro's magic shield.

"Come down and fight!" shouted Tom's enemy. One of Claw's long monkey arms arced across the sky, missing Ferno by a whisker.

"Tom!" Elenna screamed.

He looked down and saw the earth beneath his companion's feet crumbling. Elenna struggled for balance, and then fell as the ground broke open. A girl with pale skin and jet-black hair burst out from the earth, carrying a shovel.

Sethrina, Seth's sister!

The rules of this game were changing all the time.

Before Elenna could right herself, Sethrina ran across the plain and climbed up Vipero's scaly coils to sit beside her evil brother. Tom guided Ferno back to the ground and landed beside Elenna. He slid from Ferno's back to help her up. The Super-Beast began thundering towards them.

"That's cheating!" Elenna said. She grimaced as she climbed stiffly to her feet.

Sethrina sneered. "Ha! Your foolish magician may have placed a shield over the battle field, but he can't stop me digging underneath it."

"If they're going to ignore the rules, let's give them the same treatment," said Elenna. Ferno seemed to understand and extended a wing towards her. She ran up its length and Tom followed.

Now I'll do whatever it takes to win, Tom thought. He guided Ferno above their enemies.

"Too late!" called Seth, as the Super-Beast made for the plinth.

"After them, Ferno!" shouted Tom.

The Super-Beast had a head start, but its huge body lumbered along the ground, and Seth was fighting to control Trillion's three twisting heads.

"It looks like the Super-Beast may not be so great, after all," said Tom, grinning. Ferno darted after their enemies.

"Hurry, Ferno!" urged Tom. The Super-Beast extended a giant hairy arm towards the plinth. If Tom didn't get there soon…

An arrow whizzed past Tom's ear and embedded itself in Claw's limb. Trillion's three heads lifted as one, and growled

in pain. Tom twisted round and saw that Elenna had her bow in her hand.

"Great shot, Elenna!" he said.

Sethrina jumped down from the Super-Beast and sprinted towards the plinth.

Elenna smiled grimly. "You take on Seth – I'll handle his sister. If we split up it will give us an advantage."

Tom directed Ferno down towards the plain. Elenna slipped off the Beast and landed in the grass beside Storm. In one fluid movement, she was up and onto the stallion's back. She fired two more arrows at Sethrina, who ducked behind a boulder.

Seth turned his Super-Beast to face Tom. Ferno dived, blasting jets of fire from his nostrils. The smell of singed hair filled the sky as Trillion's three heads roared in anger.

Ferno landed and ran through the grass towards their enemy. As he did so, Vipero's tail whipped around, and Tom lunged to one side as it sliced the air.

Trillion sank his teeth into Ferno's wing. The dragon bellowed and staggered backwards, clouds of black smoke drifting from his nostrils. Tom couldn't hold on, and was thrown off, landing hard.

"Ferno!" he shouted.

"Seems your Beast is no match for mine," mocked Seth. One of Claw's arms was around Tom's waist before he could stand, and he was lifted high in the air.

"Kill him!" shouted Seth.

Tom could hardly breathe, and his sword arm was trapped against his side. He was being lifted towards

Trillion's gaping jaws.

"Help!" he shouted, twisting desperately to find Elenna. She was struggling with Sethrina on the ground near the plinth.

Strings of saliva stretched between the Super-Beast's jagged teeth. Tom was so close he could smell the rotten stench of Trillion's breath. He jammed his shield inside the mouth of the nearest lion head. The jaws snapped shut, and splinters flew from Tom's shield. But it held firm!

"Devour him!" yelled Seth, furiously.

Suddenly a grey streak flashed by.

Silver!

Elenna's wolf leapt into the air and sank his teeth into Claw's arm.

The three heads roared simultaneously and Tom's shield clattered to the ground.

The grip around his waist loosened and he swiped with his sword at one of Trillion's massive necks. The blade hit home, blood spurting. Tom heaved his sword free and hacked again. Shrieking, the Super-Beast released its hold and Tom plummeted to the ground.

He looked up and saw the stricken Beast swaying back and forth. Vipero's tail lashed the grass in agony. With a flick of Claw's arm, Silver was sent flying, landing in the plains twenty paces away. But the wolf sprang straight up again.

The Super-Beast collapsed to one side and the ground shook. Seth cried out from beneath the mighty weight of the three merged bodies.

"Seth!" shouted Sethrina. "Brother?"

She rushed to where the Super-Beast lay writhing in pain. Seth

wriggled out from under it. As Tom watched, mesmerised, the three bodies of the evil Beast separated once more. Claw leapt up and down, cradling his injured arm, then ran away across the plain.

"Wait!" said Seth. "Where are you going? No!"

Vipero's twin heads gaped and hissed, his tongues forking in and out. The snake man detached himself, slithering off across the plain. He dived into the hole Sethrina had dug. Tom watched as the scaly tail disappeared.

"Stop!" said Seth. "Cowards!"

Trillion bounded away and smashed through the magic rainstorm.

The Beasts had fled; the battle was over.

"Seems like your Super-Beast has

had enough," said Tom, coming to stand beside Elenna.

Sethrina looked at her brother in panic, but a slow smile crept across his lips. Doubt prickled at the back of Tom's mind.

"Now!" shouted Seth.

A shadow crept over them. Tom spun around. A great thundercloud was approaching at tremendous speed.

Silver howled, and backed away.

"What's happening?" whispered Elenna.

"I don't know," Tom hissed in reply.

It was a storm. Lightning flashed, scattering smoke and sparks through the air. Looming over them was the thick trunk of an enormous tornado, which was taller than King Hugo's castle. It swirled so fast it was a blur.

Then, gradually, a face formed in the

spinning winds – two eyes and the curl
of a sneer, from which came the
familiar sound of mocking laughter…

"Malvel!" cried Tom.

The evil wizard's voice crackled like
thunder from amidst the bruised
clouds. "Behold your doom, Tom.
I am Sephir, monster of the storm!"

CHAPTER FOUR

THE HEART
OF THE STORM

Tom ran to where Ferno was waiting.
He flung himself on the good Beast's
back.

"Climb up next to me!" he called to
Elenna. "We're dead if we try to fight
Sephir on the ground."

Seth laughed. "You think you and
your dragon are a match for Malvel's
sorcery? There's no way you can tackle
this Beast."

Elenna sprinted over and scrambled up beside Tom. Ferno thrashed his wings and they were airborne.

The air was suddenly cool as the sun disappeared behind the tornado. Sephir roared, and the sound was like a tempest at sea.

An arm made of whirling wind reached out from the body of the tornado as it drew closer. For a moment Tom thought they'd be crushed. But Ferno dodged to one side. The wind rushed past Tom, whipping up his hair as though fingers were snatching at him, threatening to drag him off the dragon's back. He gripped Ferno's scales until his knuckles were white. They rose high above Sephir's head.

"Tom, the Book!" shouted Elenna.

Oh no!

Sephir's arm closed in on the plinth, causing the Book's pages to flutter wildly. Then the Book of Worlds was snatched up. It vanished into Sephir's dark heart, and he gave a roar of triumph that sounded like a screaming gale.

"It's over," Sethrina yelled gleefully over the noise. "The Book of Worlds is Malvel's!"

Tom stared into the spinning eddies of Sephir's body. Ferno circled the tornado, batting his wings hard to avoid being drawn in by the pull of the wind.

"If only I could get inside," Tom said.

"Inside?" asked Elenna.

"Sephir's not solid like a normal Beast," said Tom. "He's just air."

Tom steered Ferno over the top of Sephir, then carefully stood up on the

dragon's back as he hovered above the tornado.

"What's your plan?" said Elenna, grabbing his arm.

"We're going into the heart of the storm. While there's blood in my veins, I won't let Malvel steal the Book of Worlds!"

Tom made sure his shield was tight across his back. It was now or never.

"Ready?" he said.

Elenna gripped his hand firmly. "Let's do this."

With his friend at his side, Tom leapt off Ferno's back and into the roaring winds below.

Sephir let out a cry of pain and anger, whipping around faster than ever before.

"No!" Tom heard Seth cry out in protest.

Tom plummeted like a rock, then turned upside down as the tornado seized him. He felt his limbs being flung about as he was spun round in the cyclone. When he managed to open his eyes, all he could see was a blur. Then he made out a shape opposite him.

Elenna!

She was pinned to the sides of the tornado, held by the sheer force of Sephir's fury. Tom felt sick with dizziness. A noise like a thousand wailing cats echoed in his ears. Sephir was in agony.

The winds writhed and turned, and it was impossible for Tom to get his bearings as they sank deeper inside. *Where's the Book?* he thought desperately.

Then suddenly the world was still.

Elenna floated beside him, cushioned on the air. He spotted the Book of Worlds being sucked through the empty space. Its gold-edged pages quivered violently and the spine was warped and broken, but the lock still held.

Tom dived after the Book, pulling himself with long strokes through Sephir's insides. The air was as chilly as a winter morning. He stretched out his fingers, and they brushed over the rough leather cover of the Book.

Almost there!

But the Book was whipped away in a sudden gust, and Sephir's laughter boomed.

"You don't have the strength," said Malvel's voice.

The cover of the Book of Worlds sprang open. Some of its pages were

ripped out, and flew off like leaves tugged from a tree in a gale.

"You've failed," said Malvel's voice. "The Book that your father almost died for is mine. All Avantia will bow before me!"

There must be something I can do, thought Tom. *This Beast must have a weakness!*

He drew his trusty blade, and with both hands on the hilt cut wide arcs through the air.

Malvel's cackle sounded again. "You can't hurt Sephir!"

Tom looked at Elenna, who was trying to grasp the torn pages of the Book of Worlds as they swirled around. He sheathed his sword.

Was it truly over? Had he let Aduro down? The air went cold again as the remaining pages spiralled away on the currents of air.

"Look, Tom!" Elenna shouted over the howling noise, pointing downwards with a stabbing gesture. "What's that?"

A blue light glowed below, right in the centre of the spiralling winds.

"I don't know," he called. "But I'm going to find out."

"The storm is more powerful down there," said Elenna. "You'll be ripped apart!"

"My golden armour will protect me," he said. The magical chainmail he had won on his Quest against Claw gave him strength of heart.

Tom turned and kicked through the raging winds. His clothes and hair streamed around him as he powered downwards. Each stroke was more difficult than the one before. The blue light became stronger, but so did the fury of the tornado.

It was like pushing through a blizzard. Tom felt ice crystals forming on his eyelashes. Thank goodness for Nanook's bell, embedded in his shield. With it, he was protected from the worst of the cold.

Tom's breath became rasping and

heavy. His heart thumped in his chest.

I won't give up, he thought. He kept his eyes fixed on the blue light. *Only a few more strokes…*

"Keep going, Tom!" called Elenna.

All around the tornado blasted him – it felt like being yanked in different directions by a hundred snatching hands. His arms burned.

Then the outer part of the blue orb shifted. In its shimmering surface, the features of a face appeared. A face

Tom would recognise until the day
he died.

Malvel.

So that was how the Dark Wizard
controlled Sephir. Malvel dwelled at
the heart of the storm, powering the
Beast with his evil.

Suddenly new blasts of wind
slammed into him, and Tom felt
his teeth rattle in his head. He was
being pushed backwards. The blue
light became blinding.

"You're not strong enough,"
Malvel's cruel voice sneered. "Sephir
will spit you out like a cherry stone."

Tom pulled his shield in front of him.

"Not this time," he said. If only he
could reach the orb. He unsheathed
his sword again.

It was now or never.

CHAPTER FIVE

THE BOOK
OF WORLDS

The wind smashed into his body like a giant invisible fist. The tornado tried to pluck his sword away, but Tom gripped the hilt until his hand throbbed. He lifted his arm above his head. Then he plunged his sword into the orb.

Tom's arm shook as energy surged up the blade. His whole body turned

hot, and the air was filled with the smell of burning.

In the centre of the orb, Malvel's sneer disappeared. The howl of the winds was replaced by a shrill scream of horror. The blue light dimmed and vanished.

The spinning gales that had gripped Tom's body released their hold, and suddenly he could see sunlight again. The storm was passing.

A scream cut through the air above, and Elenna thudded into Tom. They both plummeted to the ground, and Tom saw the plains rush up to meet them. He managed to turn and get his shield beneath him. Arcta's magical feather slowed his descent and they landed softly in the grass.

"Are you all right?" asked Tom.

"I think so," Elenna said.

A shadow fell over them and Tom
looked up. It was Storm! Tom used his
stallion's reins to help him stand, and
dusted himself down. Silver was
licking Elenna's face. Her clothes
were torn and her hair stuck up in
all directions.

"Look at Sephir!" she said.

"Come back!" shouted Seth, waving his arms angrily. The storm monster was disintegrating before their eyes. "Where are you going?"

"Sephir's given up," said Tom. "Malvel's magic was all that was pushing him on."

"You're burnt," said Elenna.

Tom felt his hair. It was crispy and stiff.

"Malvel's evil must have passed through my sword," he said. "But I feel fine."

A thud made them both spin around. There, on the plinth, sat the tattered Book of Worlds.

"Oh, Tom," said Elenna. "Look at it. It's ruined."

She was right. Hardly any pages remained. The Book was ragged and

torn and the cover was hanging off.

What have I done? thought Tom. He walked slowly to the plinth. Even the silver lock on the front was dull and scratched.

"Tom, look!" said Elenna. She was pointing upwards. Tom saw what he thought was a bird in the sky, fluttering its wings.

It was joined by another.

"Wait a moment," said Tom. "They're not birds. They're…"

"…pages!" finished Elenna.

The pieces of parchment drifted out of the clouds. The first spiralled on a breeze, then settled perfectly back into the Book of Worlds. The others joined it, each lying in its rightful place.

"It can't be!" Sethrina shouted. "What's happening?"

Elenna and Tom rushed over to the plinth.

Up close, the Book seemed to glow. Now it looked like it had never been moved.

Tom stroked the smooth leather cover and gently opened the Book. The first page was a map of Avantia, drawn in bright colours and inscribed with decorative script.

He turned it over.

"Gorgonia!" said Elenna.

Tom flicked through several more pages. Each held a map more exotic than the last. There was a map of Rion – a kingdom he had visited on a previous Quest. There were also lands he'd never heard of, let alone seen – places with names like Gwildor, Baltland and Marromore.

Could it be that each realm held Beasts of its own?

"No wonder Malvel wants the Book so badly," said Tom. "He could wreak havoc with all this information."

"Hey," shouted a voice. "Get this Beast away from us."

Seth and his sister gripped each other in terror as the fire dragon stood over them, his nostrils smoking.

"What shall we do with them?" asked Elenna. She gave Tom a wink.

"Maybe we should let Ferno toast

them," said Tom, playing along.

"No, please," said Seth. "We didn't mean any harm."

"We were just doing what Malvel told us," Sethrina added.

As much as he hated Seth and all he stood for, Tom couldn't let the pair be killed. That would make him no better than Malvel.

"Do you promise to leave Avantia and never come back?" he said.

Both nodded, looking nervously up at Ferno.

"Good," said Tom. "I'll arrange your transport." He looked at the fire dragon, who seemed to understand.

Ferno scooped the brother and sister up with his wing and dropped them onto his back. He blasted flames into the sky. Then, in three massive strides, he was airborne and beating his

powerful wings. Storm and Silver
came to stand beside Tom and Elenna,
and together they watched the Beast
disappear over the horizon.

I couldn't ask for more loyal friends,
Tom thought.

"Let's hope Ferno doesn't drop them

in the sea," said a voice.

Tom spun around and saw Aduro
stroking his long beard. In his other
hand was the Book of Worlds.

Elenna ran to throw her arms
around the good wizard.

"The battle is over," said Aduro, smiling as Elenna hugged him. "You have made Taladon proud today, Tom."

"And Avantia is safe?" asked Elenna.

"Thanks to both of you," said Aduro.

All five of them turned to gaze over the rolling hills of Avantia. Aduro tucked the Book of the Worlds under his arm and began to fade away.

"I'll return this to safekeeping, where it belongs," he told Tom and Elenna, his voice becoming faint as he disappeared. They waved goodbye. Then Tom turned to face his friend.

"Are you ready for whatever happens next? There's sure to be another Quest soon," Tom said. The sun was beginning to set over the horizon.

Elenna grinned. "I'll always be ready," she said. Silver leapt into the

air, barking, and Storm bucked his back legs. Tom laughed as he led the way over to a flat patch of ground that would make a good camp for the night.

"Then let's see what the morning brings," he said. He was certain he and his friends would be called on again.

Hc couldn't wait!